Read more DRAGON books!

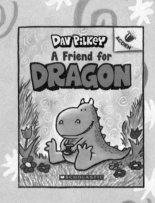

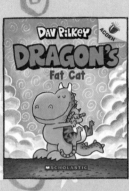

DRAGON's
Merry Christmas

DAV PILKEY

ACORN™
SCHOLASTIC INC.

For Linda and Amelie Anderson

Library of Congress Cataloging-in-Publication Data

Names: Pilkey, Dav, 1966– author, illustrator.
Title: Dragon's merry Christmas / Dav Pilkey.
Description: New York : Acorn/Scholastic Inc., 2020. | Series: Dragon ; 5 | Originally published: New York : Orchard Books, 1991. | Summary: Dragon has a merry time in the Christmas season decorating a tree outdoors, making a chocolate candy wreath, and sharing his Christmas gifts with those in need.
Identifiers: LCCN 2018046399 | ISBN 9781338347531 (hc : alk. paper) | ISBN 9781338347524 (pb : alk. paper)
Subjects: LCSH: Dragons — Juvenile fiction. | Christmas stories. | Gifts — Juvenile fiction. | Sharing — Juvenile fiction. | Friendship — Juvenile fiction. | CYAC: Dragons — Fiction. | Christmas — Fiction. | LCGFT: Christmas fiction. | Picture books.
Classification: LCC PZ7.P63123 Dt 2020 | DDC (E) — dc23
LC record available at https://lccn.loc.gov/2018046399

10 9 8 7 6 5 4 3 2 1   20 21 22 23 24

Printed in China 62
This edition first printing, October 2020
Book design by Dav Pilkey and Sarah Dvojack

Contents

1
The Perfect Christmas Tree

One cold morning, Dragon went out
to find the perfect Christmas tree.

He walked through the crunchy snow.

He saw all sorts of trees . . .
big ones, small ones,
crooked ones, and straight ones.

Finally, he found the most beautiful
Christmas tree of all.

It was not too big,
or too small.
It was not too crooked,
or too straight.
It was just right.

Dragon looked down and saw
the tree's beautiful brown trunk.
It stood firm and strong
in the frozen earth.

6

He looked up and saw
its beautiful green branches.
They waved back and forth
in the cold December wind.

Dragon could not cut down
such a lovely tree.

Instead, he came back
with colored lights, silver bells . . .

. . . and everything he needed
to make his tree even more beautiful.

11

That night, Dragon looked out
at his Christmas tree
shining in the night.
It was truly perfect.

2
The Candy Wreath

One day in December,
Dragon had a good idea.

"I will make a wreath out of candy,"
he said.

Dragon took some old wire
and bent it into shape.
Then he taped little pieces
of chocolate candy all around it.

When Dragon hung his candy wreath
on the wall, one of the pieces
of chocolate fell off.

Dragon picked it up and ate it.
It was very good.

Dragon did not want his wreath
to look bare, so he promised
not to eat any more candy.

"I will eat only the pieces
that fall off," he said.

Dragon bumped his elbow against the wall, and two more pieces of candy fell off.

"Whoops," he said, gobbling them up.

Dragon sat down in his chair
and looked up at his candy wreath.

He tried not to think about
the smooth,
rich,
sweet,
creamy,
dark chocolate candy.

Dragon could not sit still.
He began to drool.

Suddenly, Dragon could not stop himself.

He shook the candy wreath
back and forth . . .

. . . and then jumped up and down on it,
until every last piece of candy had fallen off.

Dragon got a tummy ache
from eating so much chocolate.

"Next year," said Dragon,
"I will make my wreath
out of pine cones."

3
Mittens

Dragon was always losing his mittens.
No matter how hard he tried,
he could never keep track of them.
Whenever he needed them most,
they were nowhere to be found.

So Dragon went out and bought
a pair of clip-on mittens.

He clipped them to his coat sleeves,
so he would never lose his mittens again.

Then he lost his coat.

4
Merry Christmas, Dragon

Dragon loved Christmas.
Every year he saved his money,
and every Christmas
he bought wonderful presents
for himself.

Dragon made a list of the things
he would buy.

1. Lots of food.
2. a new coat.
3. a big birdhouse.

Then Dragon wrapped himself up
in a warm quilt
and headed off to the store.

When Dragon finished his Christmas shopping,
the store clerk loaded everything into a big sack.

On his way home, Dragon passed
some raccoons singing in the street.

The raccoons had no food to eat.
They looked very hungry.

Dragon reached into his sack
and took out his big basket of food.

"Merry Christmas," said Dragon.

Then he passed an old rhino
shoveling her sidewalk.

The rhino did not have a coat to wear.
She looked very cold.

Dragon reached into his sack
and took out his new wool overcoat.

"Merry Christmas," said Dragon.

Finally, Dragon saw two little birds
sitting on a branch.

The birds did not have a home to live in.
They looked very sad.

Dragon opened his big sack,
took out his birdhouse,
and hung it on a branch.

"Merry Christmas," said Dragon.

When Dragon got home,
his big sack was empty.

There were no presents left for him.
But Dragon did not feel sad.

He went upstairs to his quiet room
and crawled beneath his soft, warm quilt.

And later, as he slept,
Dragon dreamed he heard angels
singing in the starry night.

About the Author

Dav Pilkey is the creator of the bestselling Dog Man and Captain Underpants series. He has written and illustrated many other books for young readers, including the Caldecott Honor book *The Paperboy*, *Dog Breath*, and *The Hallo-Wiener*. Dav lives in the Pacific Northwest with his wife.

YOU CAN DRAW DRAGON!

 Draw a jelly bean shape. The bottom should not connect to the top.

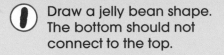 Add Dragon's eyes and nose. Put two horns on top of his head.

 Add the bottom of Dragon's mouth and his chin.

4 Draw Dragon's neck. (It is covered by his scarf.) Add his tummy.

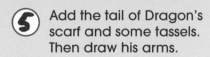 Add the tail of Dragon's scarf and some tassels. Then draw his arms.

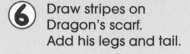 Draw stripes on Dragon's scarf. Add his legs and tail.

7 Draw spikes down his back and on his tail.

8 Color in your drawing!

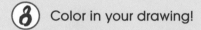

WHAT'S YOUR STORY?

Dragon donates his Christmas gifts to those in need
What would **you** donate to help those in need?
Would you help people or animals?
How would you feel after helping out?
Write and draw your story!

BONUS!

Try making your story just like Dav — with watercolors! Did you know that Dav taught himself how to watercolor when he was making the Dragon books? He went to the supermarket, bought a children's watercolor set, and used it to paint the entire book series.